MR.GRUMBLE

MR. GRUMBLE

by Roger Hargreaves

WORLD INTERNATIONAL

Mr Grumble's name suited him well!

"Bah!" he would grumble, every morning,
when his alarm clock rang.
"It's the start of yet another
horrible day!"

"Bah!" he would groan every afternoon,
on his walk in the country.
"I hate the countryside!"

One day, just after he had said this,
someone suddenly appeared by magic.

It was a wizard.

A wizard, to whom Mr Grumble had the
nerve to say, "Bah! I hate wizards who
suddenly appear by magic."

"Really?" said the wizard.
"Well, I don't like people who are constantly
grumbling and moaning. I'll tell you what
I do to people who have bad manners.
I turn them into …

… little pigs!"

And the wizard disappeared,
leaving behind him a very piggy
looking Mr Grumble.

Mr Grumble was afraid that he might
remain a pig for the rest of his life.

But five minutes later,
by magic, of course,
he changed back into his old self.

He set off again and happened to pass
Little Miss Fun's house.

"Come in!" she cried.
"I'm having a party!"

Mr Grumble went in, but when he heard
Little Miss Fun's guests singing and
laughing he scowled.

"Bah!" he moaned.
"I can't stand singing and laughing!"

He would have done better to
have kept quiet, because …

… the wizard appeared once more.

"I see that my first lesson
wasn't enough!" he said.
"If I'm going to teach you to stop grumbling,
groaning and moaning, I'll have to do
more than turn you into a little pig,
I'll have to turn you into …

… a big pig!"

Mr Grumble did not like it one bit.

Little Miss Fun and her guests, however,
found it very funny.

"Please," begged Mr Grumble,
"turn me back to normal!
I promise that I will never grumble,
groan or moan ever again!"

And he feebly wiggled his curly tail.

The wizard took pity on him,
and changed him back into his old self.

And then the wizard disappeared again.

Then Little Miss Fun jumped on to a table
and pretended to be a clown.

Mr Grumble was not amused.

"Bah!" he snorted.
"I can't stand people who jump on to tables
and pretend to be clowns!"

You can guess what happened next.

He turned into …

… an enormous pig!

An enormous pig whose face was
red with embarrassment!

"Oink!" wailed Mr Grumble, mournfully.

Then, this enormous red-faced pig,
made a solemn promise.

"Never again will I grumble, groan,
moan or snort!"

"Good," said the wizard,
suddenly appearing once again.

And Mr Grumble changed back
into his old self.

Well, not exactly his old self!

Look at that nice smile on his face.

Amazing, isn't it?

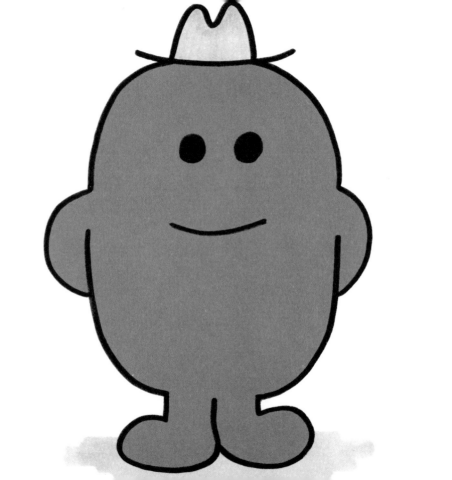

Later, Mr Grumble went home.

And, tired out after his exhausting day,
he went straight to bed.

He slept the whole night
without once grumbling,
groaning, moaning or snorting.

But not without …

… snoring!

MR MEN question time – can you help?
10 sets of 4 Mr Men titles to be won!

Thank you for purchasing a Mr Men pocket book. We would be most grateful if you would help us with the answers to a few questions. Each questionnaire received will be placed in a monthly draw – you could win four Mr Men books of your choice and a free bookmark!

Is this the first Mr Men pocket book you have purchased?   **Yes** ☑ **No** ☑ (please tick)

If No, how many books do you have in your collection?   20

Have you collected any Little Miss books?   **Yes** ☑ **No** ☑ **How many** 2

Where do you usually shop for children's books?   **Bookshop** ☑   **Newsagent** ☑
Supermarket ☑   **Garden Centre** ☑

Would you be interested in a presentation box to keep your Mr Men books in?   **Yes** ☑ **No** ☑

Do you know that there are other types of Mr Men books?   **Yes** ☑ **No** ☑

If No, would you be interested in knowing about these?   **Yes** ☑ **No** ☑

Apart from Mr Men, who is your favourite children's character? MRS MILL

Thank you for your help.

Return this form to: Marketing Department, World International Limited
Deanway Technology Centre, Wilmslow Road, Handforth, Cheshire SK9 3FB.

Please tick overleaf which four **Mr Men** books you would like to receive if you are successful in our monthly draw and fill in your name and address details.

Signature of parent or guardian:

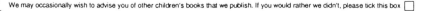

We may occasionally wish to advise you of other children's books that we publish. If you would rather we didn't, please tick this box ☐

*(left margin, vertical text)* Please remove this page carefully

Tick the 4 Mr Men books you would like to win.

☐ 1. Mr Tickle
☐ 2. Mr Greedy
☐ 3. Mr Happy
☐ 4. Mr Nosey
☐ 5. Mr Sneeze
☐ 6. Mr Bump
☐ 7. Mr Snow
☐ 8. Mr Messy
☐ 9. Mr Topsy-Turvy
☐ 10. Mr Silly
☐ 11. Mr Uppity
☐ 12. Mr Small
☐ 13. Mr Daydream
☐ 14. Mr Forgetful
☐ 15. Mr Jelly

☐ 16. Mr Noisy
☐ 17. Mr Lazy
☐ 18. Mr Funny
☐ 19. Mr Mean
☐ 20. Mr Chatterbox
☐ 21. Mr Fussy
☐ 22. Mr Bounce
☐ 23. Mr Muddle
☐ 24. Mr Dizzy
☐ 25. Mr Impossible
☐ 26. Mr Strong
☐ 27. Mr Grumpy
☐ 28. Mr Clumsy
☐ 29. Mr Quiet
☐ 30. Mr Rush

☐ 31. Mr Tall
☐ 32. Mr Worry
☐ 33. Mr Nonsense
☐ 34. Mr Wrong
☐ 35. Mr Skinny
☐ 36. Mr Mischief
☐ 37. Mr Clever
☐ 38. Mr Busy
☐ 39. Mr Slow
☐ 40. Mr Brave
☐ 41. Mr Grumble
☐ 42. Mr Perfect
☐ 43. Mr Cheerful

Your name _____

Address _____

_____

_____ Postcode _____

MORE SPECIAL OFFERS
FOR MR MEN AND LITTLE MISS READERS

In every Mr Men and Little Miss book like this one, and now in the Mr Men
sticker and activity books, you will find a special token. Collect six tokens and we
will send you a gift of your choice
Choose either a Mr Men or Little Miss poster, **or** a Mr Men or Little Miss
double sided full colour bedroom door hanger.

Return this page **with six tokens per gift required** to:

Marketing Dept., MM / LM, World International Ltd.,
PO Box 7, Manchester, M19 2HD

Your name:_____ Age: _____

Address: _____

_____

_____Postcode: _____

Parent / Guardian Name (Please Print)_____

|← 100 mm →|

ENTRANCE FEE
3 SAUSAGES

250 mm

MR. GREEDY

Please tape a 20p coin to your request to cover part post and package cost

I enclose <u>six</u> tokens per gift, and 20p please send me:-

Collect six of these tokens
You will find one inside every
Mr Men and Little Miss book
which has this special offer.

20p

Stick 20p here please

		Please Tick Appropriate Box
Posters:-	Mr Men Poster	☐ Little Miss Poster ☐
Door Hangers -	Mr Nosey / Muddle ☐	Mr Greedy / Lazy ☐
	Mr Tickle / Grumpy ☐	Mr Slow / Busy ☐
	Mr Messy / Quiet ☐	Mr Perfect / Forgetful ☐
	L Miss Fun / Late ☐	L Miss Helpful / Tidy ☐
	L Miss Busy / Brainy ☐	L Miss Star / Fun ☐

1 TOKEN

We may occasionally wish to advise you of other Mr Men gifts.
If you would rather we didn't please tick this box ☐

Offer open to residents of UK, Channel Isles and Ireland only

Full colour Mr Men and Little Miss Library Presentation Cases in durable, wipe clean plastic.

In response to the many thousands of requests for the above, we are delighted to advise that these are now available direct from ourselves,
for only £4.99 (inc VAT) plus 50p p&p.
The full colour boxes accommodate each complete library. They have an integral carrying handle as well as a neat stay closed fastener.
Please do not send cash in the post. Cheques should be made payable to **World International Ltd.** for the sum of **£5.49** (inc p&p) per box.

Please note books are not included.

Please return this page with your cheque, stating below which presentation box you would like, to:-

**Mr Men Office, World International
PO Box 7, Manchester, M19 2HD**

Your name: _Archie Holt Tom Cosslex_

Address: _____

_____

_____ Postcode: _____

Name of Parent/Guardian (please print): _Rachel_

Signature: _____

I enclose a cheque for £_____ made payable to World International Ltd.,

Please send me a Mr Men Presentation Box ☐

Little Miss Presentation Box ☐

(please tick or write in quantity) and allow 28 days for delivery

Thank you

Offer applies to UK, Eire & Channel Isles only